The Tickle Tree

Written by Chae Strathie and illustrated by Poly Bernatene

PaRragon

Bath · New York · Singapore · Hong Kong · Cologne · Delhi
Melbourne · Amsterdam · Johannesburg · Auckland · Shenzhen

Have you ever been there

...and laughed as it jiggles its twigs on your toes?.

Have you sat on the back of a giant galumph

Have you scratched an old crabbysnap under its chin

or slept through the sound of a **boomjangle's din?**

Have you walked with a **wibblebird** made out of jelly

or perched on the paunch of a **blubbalub's belly?**

If the answer is no,
then you shouldn't despair,
as I'm sure that there's some way
for you to get there.

Have you leaped like a springbungle up to the stars and said "howdy-do!" to the Grimbles on Mars?

Have you wondered why horse-riding

Or played hide-and-seek with a luminous frink?

poo-munkles stink?

To get there is simple,
but you'll have to wait
and hope that I tell you
before it's too late!

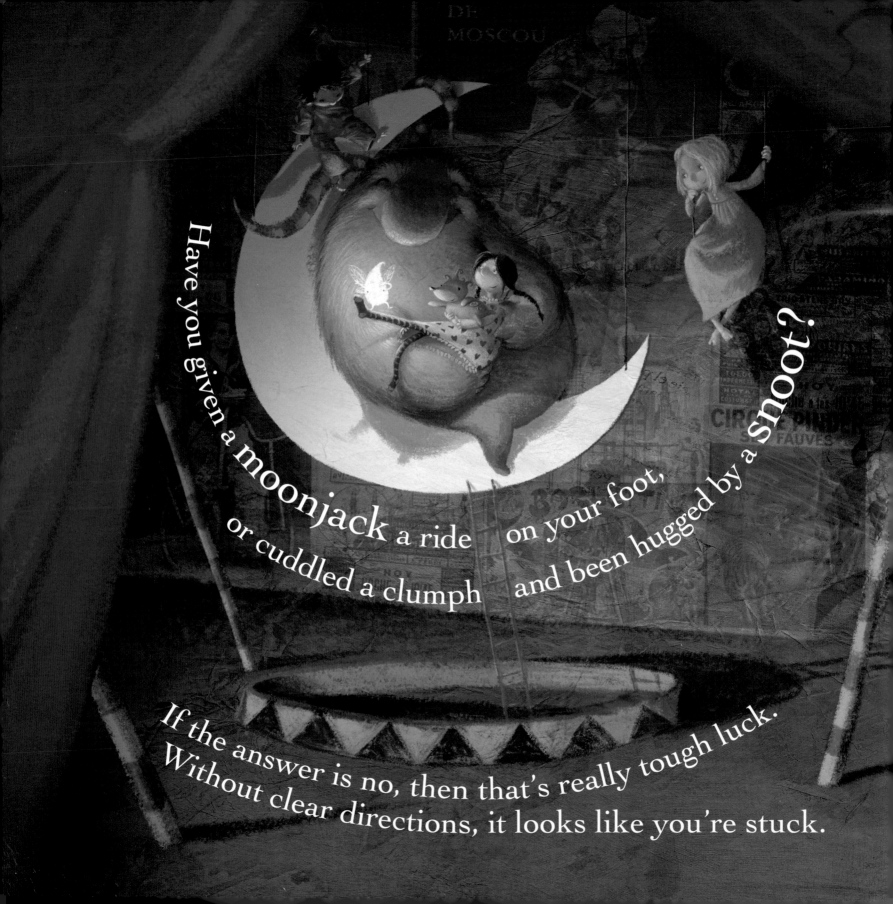

Have you given a moonjack a ride on your foot,
or cuddled a clumph and been hugged by a snoot?

If the answer is no, then that's really tough luck.
Without clear directions, it looks like you're stuck.

Have you danced with a **marvelous** musical **meep**
or dunked with a **dennyfish** down in the **deep?**

Have you had a **pink** puffalunk's last piece of pie
or climbed a free **fangdangle** up to the sky?

Don't tell me
you haven't,
I'm really surprised.

All right, then,
I'll show you, but first
close your eyes.

It's clear that you're eager to get to this place,

where snugglebugs buzz and ripunzelruns race.

I'll show you the way, but it's not where it seems.

Through the Tickle Tree's leaves and...

...into your dreams!

With love to my mum Gill
and my dad Calum,
and not forgetting Eilidh,
who's at the heart of every book.

C.S.

For my children,
who teach me how to fly...

P.B.

This edition published by Parragon in 2010

Parragon
Queen Street House
4 Queen Street
Bath BA1 1HE, UK

Text Copyright © Chae Strathie
Illustrations Copyright © 2008 Poly Bernatene
The rights of Chae Strathie and Poly Bernatene to be identified as the author and illustrator of this work have been asserted by them in accordance with the Copyright, Designs and Patents Act, 1988

Published by arrangement with Meadowside Children's Books, 185 Fleet Street, London EC4A 2HS.

ISBN 978-1-4454-0436-3

Printed in China